D0045474

Gemma & Gus

Olivier Dunrea

Houghton Mifflin Harcourt

Boston New York

The text of this book is set in Shannon.
The illustrations are pen-and-ink and gouache on 140-pound d'Arches coldpress watercolor paper.

Library of Congress Cataloging-in-Publication Data
Dunrea, Olivier.
Gemma & Gus / by Olivier Dunrea.
p. cm.
Summary: Gemma is a small yellow gosling who likes to lead and her brother is a smaller yellow gosling who likes to follow.
ISBN 978-0-547-86851-6
[1. Brothers and sisters—Fiction. 2. Geese—Fiction.] I. Title. II. Title: Gemma and Gus.
PZ7.D922Gem 2013
[E]—dc23
2012018971

Manufactured in China
SCP 10 9 8 7 6 5 4 3 2 1
4500507720

To Dani, the bravest explorer I know

This is Gemma.

This is Gus.

Gemma is a small yellow gosling.
She is the big sister.

Gus is a smaller yellow gosling.
He is the little brother.

Gemma likes to explore new places.

Gus follows.

Gemma hunts for frogs in the cattails.

Gus hunts too.

Gemma looks for bunnies hiding
in the oak tree.

Gus looks too.

Gemma hops onto the flowerpot.

Gus hops up too.

Gemma climbs on top of Molly.

Gus climbs up too.

"Don't keep following me!" Gemma honks.

Gus peeks underneath the hen.

Gemma peeks too.

Gus looks down from the flowerpot.

Gemma looks down too.

Gus jumps into the pond.

Gemma jumps too.

Gus splashes in the pond.

Gemma splashes too.

Gus scoots to a large rock.

"WHAT ARE YOU DOING?" Gemma honks.
"EXPLORING!" honks Gus.

This is Gemma.

This is Gus.

Gemma and Gus are two small goslings
who like to explore—together.